W9-AAW-487

For Jarrett, Gina, Zoe, Lucia, Xavier & Pugs Krosoczka,
and for Ember, the original idea-sparker
—S. B.

For the most important turds in my life:
Jen, Jacen, Logan, and Penny
—M. G.

Henry Holt and Company, *Publishers since 1866*
Henry Holt® is a registered trademark of Macmillan Publishing Group, LLC
120 Broadway, New York, NY 10271 • mackids.com

Text copyright © 2020 by Samantha Berger
Illustrations copyright © 2020 by Manny Galán
All rights reserved.

Library of Congress Cataloging-in-Publication Data is available
ISBN 978-1-250-23787-3

Our books may be purchased in bulk for promotional, educational, or business use.
Please contact your local bookseller or the Macmillan Corporate and Premium Sales Department at
(800) 221-7945 ext. 5442 or by email at MacmillanSpecialMarkets@macmillan.com.

First edition, 2020
The illustrations in this book were created using Adobe Photoshop CS3;
real mixed media, including pencil, paper, and acrylic; and a mercurial Wacom Cintiq.
Printed in China by Hung Hing Off-set Printing Co. Ltd., Heshan City, Guangdong Province

3  5  7  9  10  8  6  4  2

# THE GREAT BIG POOP PARTY

YOU'RE INVITED!

written by Samantha Berger        illustrated by Manny Galán

**Henry Holt and Company**

New York

**W**hen Julian's big birthday was coming up, his parents made a big announcement.

"You can have any party theme you want this year — superheroes, skateboards, dogs, anything! The choice is yours."

Julian didn't even need
to think about it.

"Poop," he declared. "It's
gonna be a poop party."

Julian's parents looked at each other.
"Um, a poop party?" asked his mother.
"A poop party," said Julian.

"How about dinosaurs? Or outer space? Or silly mustaches?" asked his dad.

"Poop," said Julian.

"Ewwwwwwww,"
said his big sister, Lily.
"Pooooooop?"

"Poop," said Julian for
the fifth time. His mind
was made up.

Julian's parents were a little bit concerned. "Uh, are people going to be okay with a poop party?" his mom asked.

"I'm not sure how anything good can come from this idea," said his dad.

"It's SOOOOOOOO GROSS," Lily said.

"You said it was my choice," said Julian. "And I want poop."

Julian's family always tried to keep their promises.

So they all went to the party store . . . in search of the poopiest party supplies they could find.

At the party store, they found

brown balloons,

brown streamers,

brown paper plates,

brown cups,

brown straws,

brown napkins,

and a smiling brown
donkey piñata.

"Aw, I thought they would have more poop stuff," said Julian.

"You know what?" said Dad.
"*I* know what," said Mom.

"*WE* know how to make better poop party stuff than this!" they both said.

"We do?" asked Julian.
"We *DO-DOO*!" said his parents. "Let's put our poopy heads together and make the best poop party ever!"

Back at home, the whole family got
to work making poop party invitations.
The invites looked GREAT.
It started to seem like something
good might come from this idea.

"If we really want to get into the poopy party spirit, we will need poop costumes," said Dad.

So the whole family made poop costumes together, with matching poop party hats.

Then they made enough for the whole party.

When the pugs put on their poop party hats, no one could stop laughing.

The day before the big poop party . . .

Dad baked
poop cupcakes.

Mom made
*poop*sicles.

Julian invented a
poop beanbag toss.

5  00  2

Lily made a
Pin-the-Poop-on-
the-Toilet game.

Dad made paint-your-own poop posters.

Mom made the smiling donkey piñata into a smiling poop piñata.

Lily made poop confetti.

Julian made poop slime.

Finally, the big day arrived. But who would actually come to a big poop party?

**EVERYONE!**

All Julian's friends,
all their parents,
Grandma, Grandpa, cousin Phyllis,
all the neighbors,
all their dogs,
teachers,
librarians,
DJ Grand Master Splash,

and even the local news team
from Channel 2, who caught
wind of the Great Big Poop Party.

A band called Dookie-Poo played, and all the kids danced dances like the Flush-Flush, the Ploppity-Plop, the Doo-Doo Doo-op,

DOOKIE-POO

SKID MARK

POOPIE!

the Code Brown, the Deuce Is Loose, the Pop-a-Squat, and the Party Pooper.

Even the kids who never usually danced, DANCED.

Everyone played poop games and whacked at the poop piñata until it exploded, from the hindquarters, with chocolate brown nuggets and lolly*poops*.

Then everyone took photos in the birthday photo *pooth*.

It was one of the greatest parties in history.

Afterward, Julian, Lily, Mom, and Dad were POOPED.

They wrote and illustrated stories about it and shared them with the class.

Then they made poop sculptures, which were so inspired, they stayed on display for a whole month.

The sculptures weren't just masterpieces — they were master*poops*!

At recess, the kids remembered the dances from the party—and made up new ones like the Potty Shuffle, the Yard Doody, and the Pooperman!

Even the principal, who never usually danced, DANCED.

The local news team ran their story on the Great Big Poop Party, and the story was shared and shared and shared.

BOY HAS POOP PARTY **2**

Suddenly the whole world was hearing about the Great Big Poop Party . . .

**MILO**
@milo

**Poop Party?**
8:50 PM
230,328 Followers

and everyone wanted to throw a poop party of their very own!

Penny 📌 KEEP

POOP PARTY? 💩 ❤️

BOY HAS POOP PARTY

**Panda Bear**
@Panda

3:30 PM
12,197 Followers

Julian and Lily and Mom and Dad wrote a "How to Throw Your Own Poop Party" comic. Julian and Lily drew the pictures. They all agreed it was some of their best work to date.

Who knew so much good could come from making a Great Big Poop Party?

Julian did.

He knew all along.

# RECIPES FOR YOUR OWN GREAT BIG POOP PARTY!

## POOP SLIME

### YOU WILL NEED:

- a glass bowl
- 1 4-oz. bottle of clear or white glue (must contain BPH)
- ½ t. baking soda
- food coloring
- a big spoon
- 1 bottle of contact saline solution
- baby oil (optional)

### DIRECTIONS:

1. In a glass bowl, pour in ½ cup of glue. (That's the whole bottle!)

2. Add baking soda and a few drops of food coloring. If you don't have brown food coloring, experiment by mixing different colors until you get the shade you want. Just remember, a teensy bit of food coloring goes a LONG way!

3. Stir that all together.

4. Time to activate the poop slime! Add one or two squirts of contact solution, then mix.

5. Squirt a little more solution; mix a little more. Repeat until it's done: when the mixture sticks together, but not to the sides of the bowl.

6. If you want, add a weensy bit of baby oil so it doesn't stick to your hands.

7. Now your poop slime is ready. Have the slime of your life!

# POOP-BEER FLOATS

## YOU WILL NEED:

- 1 mug
- root beer
- chocolate ice cream
- 1 icing bag with a tip

## DIRECTIONS:

1. Let the ice cream soften at room temperature until it is scoopable but not melted.

2. Fill a mug with root beer, leaving some space at the top.

3. Plop a scoop of chocolate ice cream into an icing bag and pipe a poop-like spiral on the surface of the root beer.

4. As you pipe, sing (to the tune of "Where Is Thumbkin?"):

   *Pour the poop beer*

   *Pour the poop beer*

   *Then you stop*

   *Then you stop*

   *Swirl and swirl the poopy*

   *Swirl and swirl the poopy*

   *On the top*

   *On the top*

5. Raise your mug, yell, "TO POOP PARTIES!" and sip.